CHILDREN'S HOSPICE

A nightmare

by

JOE GARDNER

From a story developed with

DANNY TOMLINSON

© Joe Gardner 2014

Also by Joe Gardner

The Life and Loves of Jet Tea
Oh, Vienna! (And Other Stories)

For all Winter Flowering Pansies,
past and present
For Alex, for letting me use the piano stool
For Danny and Ellie. Thanks for listening.

"If I were a thousand times more intelligent, and if I were a thousand times more beautiful, then maybe I could be her, but as it stands I have to make do with simply being with her, which is hardly a poor compromise."

"Eurgh! A spider!"

I

Little baby Christmas Rudolph picture postcard tinsel snow and cakes tasty dusty cakes warm fire pretty bow and tinsel tinsel tinsel fire cake and fucking wine elves Santa cheerful little Christmas baby smiles and songs and the turkey isn't done but Quality Street and Roses and fucking wine and Santa time and celebrations (and Celebrations) here bring the little baby open your eyes little baby open your presents little baby little baby see his little smile joy joy joy fucking eh! It's little baby Christmas Victor baby little Victor see little baby Victor one year old today! Christmas puppy yay!

Hoist him to the Heavens parade him around the room mummy pass him to daddy take him by the armpits and wave him hither, and thither, and this way, and that way, and point him at the door and thrust him at the television and spiral and swirl and lift him high and show him the tree and feed him the breadstick and dance and skip and hold the little baby tightly and waltz and stride and own the stage with little baby Victor laughing in your hands, laughing at the new world spiralling in midair and now wind down and bend your knees and slink to the floor and place the lovely baby boy delicately on the soft warm carpet for here is his rustling Christmas gift and it must be received.

And little baby Victor fiddles with the pretty bow and the shiny paper on the warm carpet floor under the lovely Christmas tree and tears at the surprise and giggles and smiles and fiddles and smiles and wriggles and miles and miles of torn, shiny paper flutter and billow out from little baby Victor's little baby palms and strew all over the merry merry Christmas carpet and out from the surprising wriggling shiny mass of shreds and bows wags and wallops and flops and lollops out little Christmas puppy yay!

Little baby Victor claps and gurgles and the Christmas puppy dances and flips and spins and wags and yips and sniffs and runs around the warm merry merry Christmas carpet and oh look at the lovely tree isn't it lovely? The lights and the angels and the tinsel and the shiny chocolate pennies and the snowmen and the stars and the beads and the plastic reindeer and the wooden elves and the plush Santa and I don't know about the pink hippo I suppose that was nan's contribution and the baubles and the candles and the gold and the green and the pines and the red and all of the gorgeous sparkly merry Christmas tree and beneath the tree fluttering and yipping and pawing the adorable the warm the new arrival the Christmas puppy yay!

And Jesus.

Get the camera dad! Get the camera dad! See little baby Victor now he's small and good and true and his little baby brain isn't pierced by hate and fear and regret get the camera and film little baby Victor and the Christmas puppy yay! See him play! Glorious day! No dismay! Christmas puppy yay!

Daddy gets the camera daddy bends his knees daddy points the big thing at little baby Victor and little baby Victor waves and gurgles and bounces on his bottom on the warm merry merry Christmas carpet and mummy claps and smiles and sips her fucking wine and watches little baby Victor through the filter of the lens the glaring neon shiny flat screen even littler little baby Victor is a star character in the centre of the frame and mummy loves to laugh and smile and the music plays on (WHAM MARIAH CAREY BONEY M even JONAH LEWIE) and the living room is warm and there are dusty cakes and Quality Streets and breadsticks and all manner of dip and chocolates to the rafters and cold beer for daddy and fucking wine for mummy and Little Baby Victor: The Movie is still in production as the Christmas puppy (yay!) flits and darts in and out of televised immortality and mummy watches the little camera screen pretend to be her little baby Victor on this glorious Christmas day - Christmas puppy yay!

Bedtime after the film for little baby Victor and the pooped out tuckered out yawning cream crackered Christmas puppy lay down in its fluffy little pit to experience Boxing Day for the first time in its arguably unnecessary existence while little baby Victor sleeps and dreams what babies dream if babies dream perhaps as perceived babies can't dream if they are creatures of instinct what could babies dream about? If a baby were brain-dead how would you know? Without medical assistance at least ponders mummy but never mind that today of all days: Christmas puppy yay!

And *Jesus.*

It was not always this way. This idyllic Christmas day preceded annually by the former festive day. That was the day upon which little baby Victor – then known only as little baby – came into being. He gestated for the best part of the year inside mummy's tummy – a child in appearance but really just larva stewing in human broth nourished by the fleshy tube and cocooned out of all spatial awareness by the flesh-egg that is growing mummy – the conduit for all of little baby's future fallibility where daddy's nine-month-passed euphoric release signalled the passing of his accountability.

It is eight months and twenty-seven days since the blissful twilit sweaty creation of little baby and the snow doesn't fall but the darkness rolls in more frequently now and the shops hang up their lights and hoist up their plastic trees and put red hats on their melancholic workers and pump SHAKIN' STEVENS through their aisles and the waddling mums and head scratching dads flock panicked to those aisles where SHAKIN' STEVENS' glittering salutations of merriment do little to soften their jittery snatches and grabs of all the best toys for all their little baby boys and girls but mummy floats glacially through the cold and the decorated dark clutching the weight of the future in her veined and strained hands for this little baby is on His way (yes they knew the sex) and it could be today it could have been yesterday but if life goes to plan it will be tomorrow – and Christmas for mummy will be back ache and blood loss and bent knees and latex-clad stranger's hands and wincing and screaming and sweating and straining and pushing and shitting and crying and sleeping and waking and loving and mummy knows this as she puffs and pants in the icy high street wondering what she is doing out tonight for the shops are all full and she dare not go inside lest she suffer the elbows and pushchairs of her would-be frantic company who'd probably bound intently toward the spot upon which she would stand – blind to her occupation of it – and in their intent would fling mummy like an unwelcome spider into the clattering shelves of the socks and pants aisle. No this is not a night mummy wishes for so she shuffles home clutching little baby wrapped in His bulbous cocoon awaiting His grand entrance into the cold world. And she is home and there is smiling daddy who places his paper on the coffee table and rises to take mummy in his arms and help her sit down for although the solitary walk in the long cold street was accomplished without aid it would be unseemly to allow his beloved and bearer of his boy to cross the room to the settee unassisted. And so he helps and mummy huffs and mummy sits and mummy's heart pumps and pumps and the active blood slurps through her swirling veins and the goodness and the iron and the nutrition canons into the tubes that feed the throbbing little kicking baby and as He is fed His eyelids rise and His eyes have flames inside them and He sees the flesh and the fluid and the amniotic debris that floats around Him and He knows where He is and He knows where He should be. It is time to live little baby! See the light my child! See the Earth! And the midnight bell chimes and it is Christmas day and mummy gasps and out comes her hand and into daddy's forearm sink her sudden claws and she gasps and leans and there is a flourish in her lap and out it leaks and it heralds His arrival and mummy knows and daddy knows that little baby will be a Christmas baby as was foretold.

Darkness streaks by and green blue purple red yellow orange pink white gold streams of light rush past beyond the glare of the steamy window. Mummy is on cold leather as the wriggling creature animates her insides and scuttles closer to her thighs and daddy drives and it's going to be alright and on the hill ahead under the black sky the white temple – the star in the sky – the glowing green cross marking out its refuge daddy spins the wheel and swerves and the tyres screech and burn and mummy is lifted and the cold nips her skin and the baby slithers within and the door is slammed and she is taken by strangers and thrown onto a mattress in a small room and it's going to be alright little baby is coming push! Push! Push! Breathe! Take daddy's hand squeeze and strain and grind your teeth and push and bleed and the little baby's fingers grip the walls and the little baby pulls and shuffles and crawls and slithers to the light and passes through mummy who roars from the strain and the little baby blinks in the overwhelming glare and sees all the wide-eyed smiles and the white walls and the blood-speckled sheets and the parted knees and he is taken by mighty hands and hoisted into the room and his coiling belly-chain is hacked apart by a glinting blade and so seeps the newborn mucus onto the mattress and this is not the world little baby had in mind and so all he can do is screw up his face and cry. Mummy, have yourself a merry little Christmas baby. And mummy cries and daddy cries and even the relatively jaded nursing staff shed a tear and on that Christmas morning the walls of the welcoming hospital cry and they are crying to this day.

And newborn little baby is taken home and named Victor and the bubble of a little life takes his bewildered soul somehow to being the one year old little baby Victor who received the little yipping puppy on that blissful Christmas day. And one year old little baby Victor goes – not without some trial and error and the occasional runny nose – to being two year old little baby Victor and all the long year mummy is nearby to hold and love and warm and kiss and teach and protect and feed and change and cuddle little baby Victor, mummy's boy child born on Christmas day. On days he plays on nights sleeps tight on days on the soft warm carpet and with the soft warm Christmas puppy and on nights in mummy's arms and sometimes the cheeky little boy crawls up onto mummy's sleeping face and mummy wakes and starts and laughs and little baby Victor laughs and not yet amply rested daddy stirs and turns and groans and shrugs indignant at the wayward child, the tearaway and the good man is losing the patience of being, or was he ever even there? Fatherhood truly makes a man himself. On days mummy stands by the piano and fiddles with the keys making tunes for little baby Victor to laugh and clap to and little baby Victor sits on the piano stool which by rights should be mummy's seat but she cares not when that super little baby's big eyes beam up to hers and the music floats on through the soft spot on his baby head (those kids are each born with such a hole there and little baby Victor's just won't fill in damn it all) and she smiles and sometimes cries her boy her joy a greater melody than ever she created on that piano (yes daddy helped but damn it all if he knows it these days) and she waits again for the nights and cheeky chappy Victor's nocturnal climb onto mummy's face to wake her up and now it is Christmas all over again where did the long year go? And them dogs don't them dogs grow up fast? Oh what did we do daddy? That little Christmas puppy will be dead at the prime of Victor's childhood. Will be cold in its pit when little baby Victor is barely through his first decade. What did we do? Why did we get that wretched mutt at such a time in our golden precious prize special gorgeous little baby Victor's little life?

Shut it woman don't be absurd that dog is two years old still laying turds in the kitchen let's leave the worry for a few years shall we? See how Christmas puppy skips and jumps and wags and yips and rolls over and over upon the ground all of the day and watches the birds in the garden and the dogs in the field and longs to gallop with them but don't we know he's a terror and can't be trusted beyond the ensnaring realm of the leash so shut it woman that wretched mutt will burden us yet Victor will deal when Victor must deal so shut it woman don't be absurd you've had too much of that fucking wine this Christmas day. Perhaps the turkey needs a look? Perhaps you've carrots yet to cook? Perhaps read some more of your book but shut it woman I need to watch this film the telly aint half as good in the long year as it is on this Christmas day and that dog will sniff our wrinkled toes in the end and that dog might even watch one of us go under the ground before it's his turn. So go and chop that bird for I am hungry and you are drunk and I have no desire to be solitary in an audience for needless fretting.

    Mummy swirls out of the room and leaves behind angry daddy and his glaring screen to which all his focus returns and she is in the unlit kitchen now and there is the fat pink bird on the side – flesh and bone and veins and vessels and dripping blood and leaking oils and seeping fats onto the metal tray with shrivelled leathery hog slices strewn across its plucked torso it lies legs parted on its back severed wing stubs splayed out at its sides exposed for the forced entry of onion and sage and more hacked hunks of hog and drunk mummy has no desire to feed this corpse to fat daddy anymore for fat daddy has said cold words and nothing more should pass those hateful lips tonight so mummy clutches the cleaver and hacks away. She strikes at the bone and it crunches in two, she strikes at the flesh and it splits and globules of congealed blood are spat out by the force of the cleaver as the cold pink skin is severed and some strike mummy's cheeks and others merely coil up mummy's knuckles and the body of the bird is flayed and diced and decimated and through all the heavy strikes of the cleaver mummy scowls back through the room and there is daddy on the chair, illuminated by the screen, his greasy hair giving wide berth to the pale, flaky bald spot on his head, a white whirlpool of resentment and coldness yawning malevolently back at mummy who chops and hacks and slices and dices and whacks at the mangled bird corpse, now just gnarled, pink chunks of bacteria-infested flesh and smeared red blood on the metal tray there will be no bird to eat on Christmas day Victor can have his baby mush daddy can have nothing but that glaring screen, ample nourishment for fat, chilly hate. And she stares at him and somehow she recalls a summer time when daddy took her hand and showed her things and there were shouts of promise and garlands of hope and blossoming forever and laughter and embraces and kissing and no forethought of the cold mangled bird or the white flaky bald spot and when daddy gives his bi-annual thought of mummy he dimly recalls his bygone mantra *she will challenge me because she is a genius and she is hilarious and she reads clever books and if I were a thousand times more intelligent and if I were a thousand times more beautiful then maybe I could BE her but as it stands I have to make do with simply being WITH her which is hardly a poor compromise* but there is no such thought tonight. No, nor is there even the thought of the absence of the thought. There is simply no thought.

What is this you stupid slut!

It is the bird daddy.

This can't be! This won't feed me!

It is all you deserve daddy.

It's Christmas day! This is my Christmas feast! What have you done to it?

It is still meat. You can still eat.

You've hacked it to bits!

I've hacked it to bits.

You're drunk!

I am drunk.

Mummy lets the cleaver go and down it clangs on the kitchen floor. Daddy raises both his hands and wipes his sad fat face and roars. His Christmas day, his day of peace, that stupid slut has chopped it to bits like the cold quivering bird now merely mangled hunks on the metal tray. This is no way to treat a man on Christmas day – go to bed Victor mummy and daddy must talk Merry Christmas little baby Victor we love you don't we mummy? Don't we cherish his little heart and all his innocent love and all the promise for your long life little baby Victor you are our golden treasure and Christmas day will always be a special day a special day for you the best day your favourite day but right now please to bed it's beddy-byes time our little love mummy and daddy love you so. There are stars that shine on you when the night rules and there is the rising sun that will hold and love you when the day has come. Goodnight little baby sleep so well we'll tuck you in soon and whisper wishes for flights of angels and the man in the moon to rockabye your tired soul into the serenity of sleep – Now he is in bed woman I can deal with you. One more act like the debacle with the bird and hell itself will freeze over before you're able to bear another son you mark my words.

Some more fucking wine for crying mummy, for daddy at his telly can't be suppressed out of her mind any other way all there is to do is drink and play the little piano at the little stool upon which little baby Victor won't sit tonight for he is the banished accessory to the crime of daddy's absence. Oh if he were truly absent this would be a happy home but his vacancy is just of the heart and this is a hell house now (what a difference a year makes), father turned his back on little baby Victor his creation and mummy can't ignore that and that is why she hacked the bird. She plays and the Christmas puppy yips and with each chime and each yip daddy winces and flinches and tenses and grinds his teeth for this is not the soundtrack to his cherished seasonal television no this is an intrusion this is an affront this is a sensory revolution and he is the monseigneur the aristocracy the decadent emperor of this family house of cards which is destined to fall as all empires must.

Leave it you stupid slut! Mummy plays on.

Put an end to that hideous tune! Christmas puppy yips on.

I'll chop that wretched thing to bits! The melody lingers on.

Well then you deaf whore feel my fist! And the music stops.

Daddy swipes and mummy bawls and mummy bites and daddy recoils and daddy strikes and mummy falls and Christmas puppy yaps and growls and the fucking wine bottle tumbles to the carpet and daddy takes hold of the zip on his fly for fatherhood has left little room for mummy and daddy time these days and now here is an angry hungry man who lunges and mummy screams.

And upstairs beneath the shade of the sweet night time and beneath the soft glow of plastic stars precious little baby Victor smiles through his baby dream and his little eyes are closed and the twinkle of innocence lullabies him safely through the peaceful slumber. Today has gone to bed but tomorrow is still dreaming and it will arise with the glowing sun which will shine through the winter and make all its dreams true and take you carefully in its arms and usher you, little baby Victor, usher you along on a golden adventure just like it has done every day of your little life.

But crash!
And bang!
And oh that sound!
Oh that's mummy!
Oh that's daddy!
It's still Christmas day!
And they laugh yet and they play!
I want to see mummy laugh!
I want to see daddy play!

Baby Victor stirs and smiles and gurgles and climbs the climb.

I want to see mummy laugh!

I want to see daddy play!

And maybe, just maybe, a warm cuddle from my Christmas puppy, yay!

So little baby Victor lands on his little baby feet and waddles excitedly to the door and its crack of big light seeping through the bottom – come into the light little baby Victor, come toward the light.

There is gnashing and grunting and gouging and thrusting and wagging and barking and flailing and crying and pushing and swiping and bleeding and sweating and crashing and screaming and roaring and kicking and smothering and ravaging and the plethora rolls on round eternal. Mummy will retaliate and daddy will pacify and mummy's defeated arms fall back to the warm warm merry Christmas carpet so daddy can continue the plunge and the dreaded plethora rolls on round eternal but mummy sees a way to be free. There on the ground beside me! That fucking wine bottle! Drained of its fucking wine! Daddy does not know it is there! For he is too busy with me!

Mummy reaches for the fucking wine bottle and takes it in her hand and, though the hunched fat frame of thrusting daddy stifles the endeavour she swings the bottle over and there and then the big door opens and out peeks the little face of little baby Victor all excited and glowing like tomorrow's sun and through the air the bottle goes and it twists and it turns and it flies and it has missed daddy but the confusion has halted his attack and he looks and he sees and he says Victor! And the bottle spins and tumbles and descends and rollicking billowing sinewy streaming black despair pours out into the air with a deafening crash and a sickening crunch the rocketing bottleneck sinks into the baby soft spot flesh brain-skull hole and back out it pings from the fleshy trampoline and down He goes with all His promise little baby Victor goes limp on the warm carpet and the fucking wine bottle rolls away from its deed and Christmas puppy barks and daddy pulls away and scarpers and cowers and puts his weapon hurriedly away and mummy is dazed on the same ground as her boy and she bends her knees and cocks her head and waits for sense and there is little baby Victor by the door, on the floor, he is not moving, he is not laughing, his eyes are not alight, open your eyes little baby, open your eyes little baby, open your eyes little baby. And daddy shrieks and mummy shrieks and Christmas puppy shrieks and on that Christmas night the house of the family Victor shrieks and it is shrieking to this day.

II

Through rigid, clasping fingers and straggled strands of twined hair from the corner of the room from the sweat of the carpet through the pounding of the chest the aching throb of the groin the shivering skin the rocking torso the heaving shoulders and the streaming tears mummy sees what little she may see. Daddy is cowered at the walls palm on the ground arm at the plaster clutching nothing sitting upright and rocking and rocking and breathing wide eyed and dishevelled and mouth agape with no intention to ever close again and mummy sees what little she may see. Christmas puppy is quaking at the door a hissing whimper emanating from its throat its shuddering knees bent its tail ceased wagging and recoiled between its back legs its eyes terrified its snout whimpering its ears flaccid and mummy sees what little she may see. Tiny hands with fingers curled not quivering or whimpering or shaking or quaking like daddy or Christmas puppy but still. Little arms protruding from little cloth pyjamas little legs draped across the carpet little toes pointing at the ceiling no animation no stirring no rise nor fall of the little chest no slight twinge of the little knees no sudden turn of the little head no opening of the little eyes little baby Victor beside the empty fucking wine bottle which only now does mummy recall sinking into his little head and felling the tiny baby boy and ceasing naughty daddy's passionate attack and mummy sees what little she may see and daddy says what little he may say.

You stupid slut! You stupid, stupid, stupid little slut! You horrific whore! You cruel cunt! You brain-dead bitch! What did you do? What did you do? Look at the little boy! Look at Victor! Laying there! You drunken wretch! Why did you wind me up? Why didn't you leave me be watching the TV? You provoked me! And you murdered that boy! Look at him! Look at his tiny corpse you stinking, honking dunce! You murdering witch! Why didn't you gouge out your cunt tubes when your had the chance? Why did I let you bring this misery into the world? Look at him! Look at your deed! You did this! I can't be blamed for acting on impulse! You brought that out of me! You threw the fucking wine bottle! You bashed the piano keys during my hour of peace!

You gave him that baying little mutt! You did all of this!

And mummy bellows and through twisted and tangled strands of sweaty hair rocks on the spot and claws at her eyes as daddy's lies his monstrous lies cut into her and little baby Victor lies still by the door and the Christmas puppy howls at daddy's spite and his knees cease quaking and he arches his back and sniffs at the air and trots cautiously to Victor's little body and buries his nose into Victor's throat and sniffs and pokes and the baby head flops to the side at the dog's activity and Christmas puppy wags and sniffs and licks Victor's little cheeks and mummy groans to behold and daddy gags and shields his eyes as the dog paws and prods and the body shifts and shuffles. But Christmas puppy wags and them dogs don't them dogs know things? Don't they have instincts we don't possess? Why Christmas puppy didn't half love that baby boy and it stands to reason he wouldn't exude such disrespect as to lick and sniff and poke his cold corpse so maybe it aint so cold and maybe it aint a corpse and Christmas puppy knows it and mummy starts to know it and daddy shielding his eyes and scratching his sinful groin maybe even he might know it little baby Victor is alive!

Daddy scrambles first. Let Me See My Boy! Mummy claws at the air. No Leave Him Alone! Daddy finds his feet and bounces to the boy and mummy shuffles on her knees and swipes for the body. He's Dead! *He's Alive!* I Killed Him! *You Missed!* You Attacked Me! *You're My Wife!* He's Dead! *He's Alive!* Mummy's hand claps around little baby Victor's ankles and she drags him toward her but daddy's grasp is on little baby Victor's crown and he pulls the other way. And a veritable tug-o-war ensues between mummy and daddy as oblivious baby Victor – be he dead, be he alive – is lifted into the air and pulled and stretched back and forth. His eyes are closed and his arms flop below him as mummy and daddy struggle. Christmas puppy yaps and growls and hops around the furore and wags from the monstrous excitement of it all. Aint he a little scamp? *Let Him Go!* You Let Him Go! *Shut Your Gob You Murderer!* You Said He's Not Dead! A bony crack is heard somewhere about Victor's stringy body and mummy hears it and daddy hears it and both recoil and daddy says *Eurgh!* And each loosen their grip neither expecting the other to do the same and so little baby Victor falls back to the ground for a second time that Christmas barely minutes after his first fall.

With the bump of baby's landing mummy grabs her hair and screams and daddy wipes his eyes he knows something we think he must know something – an inkling of concern that this may be his fault stirs in a dusty backroom of his mind perhaps the same one in which he keeps his bygone mantra of love *She will challenge me... If I were a thousand times more intelligent... I could BE her...*

Hardly a poor compromise... And like his thoughts of past mummy he shakes it out of being but by Christ's blood and bones don't we know it will be back later?

You'll be imprisoned for this! Mark my words! You did this to my son! Is he breathing? I'm getting the law! And the doctors! He will live! I promise you! *He Will Live!*

Mummy is a hurricane of sweat, tears and hair spiralling on the carpet and daddy makes good on his promise which to be honest he has been doing all day. He takes the phone and he tearfully confesses all of mummy's deeds and he tactfully omits his part in the strife and mummy hears all but listens to none and still she swirls and in the palms of her hands which mask her face at this time she sees the fucking wine bottle sinking into her baby's brain she sees the nosy Christmas puppy poking at the head and causing it to flop the side she sees hers and daddy's struggle with the little body she hears the crack and she sees it tumble and before she knows it the doorbell rings and the door is opened and daddy says Please! In Here! And in walks a medical man with a jacket that glows like all the festive promise with yellow and green reflecting the Christmas tree lights and he looks accusingly at mummy and he looks disgustedly at little baby Victor. Then back to mummy. Then back to Victor. Then he kneels before mummy on the ground and looks her in the eye with the vengeful judgement of the Heavenly

Father and mummy can hear him before he speaks. She looks up from her Christmas daydream just in time to see the new arrival drag little baby Victor's little body across the ground.

Mummy says Help Him. But the man simply lifts the baby's body up by the head and thrusts it angrily into mummy's damp face to show her as though it is dog mess and she the dog.

Look What You Did! He shakes the baby at her and its little arms and legs wiggle and dance in midair and he thrusts it in closer. Look What You Did! His enraged dark eyes peer out behind the dancing baby. This Was A Little Life! You Know What This Boy Could Have Been? We'll Do What We Can But You Should Have All The Violent Retribution Mankind Can Dream Up Heaped Upon You As Swiftly As Can Be. I'm not the lawman the lawman is outside I'm just the medic but Lord if I were the lawman I know what I'd do with you.

He pulls the baby back toward his own face and stares at it intently for a number of seconds. Then he thrusts it back at mummy with his rigid fingers almost piercing little baby Victor's delicate skull. Look At Him! Poor Little Soul! The police are outside and they're going to take you to where you belong oh what a thing to happen on Christmas day! I have two boys and as God above will attest my wife and I love them dearly and they're growing lads the oldest is now twelve and we've never hurt a hair on his head and they're at home right now waiting for daddy to come back to them I had to leave my loving family on Christmas day to deal with the work of you, you monster. Christ if there were fewer demon-whores like you on this Earth then good men like me and your poor husband over there might just get through this life in peace. I'm here to clean up your mess we'll do what we can not for you but for this boy and that man and when you're safely out of the way we can all only pray that those two suffering bastards will have a happy and peaceful life together She's In Here Officer now you want to stop that sobbing the lawman will see right through it you heinous harlot Just Through Here hmmm this baby is brain-dead I reckon. Brain-dead baby! How would you know? A brain-dead baby's brain wouldn't grow but I've seen brain-death at all ages and let me tell you they all spit and cry and gurgle like babies do irrespective of the states of their brains. Brain-dead baby! How would you know? A brain-dead man doesn't act like a man but a brain-dead baby dribbles and shits itself and gurgles just like a real baby. We'll do what we can but I think it's the Children's Hospice for this one. It's where the kiddies beyond help go to live out the last precious few hours or days or weeks or months but certainly not years of their lives. It's a foul place full of dark and leaks and creaks and ghosts and day-in-day-out it smells like rotten fish but they do look after the kiddies there.

As the dark blue officer arrives the medic hoists limp little baby Victor up into the air and takes him by the ankles and drapes him over the shoulder like an unneeded jumper as he strides out into the night shouting Hospice For This One Chaps. This One Aint Waking Up.

Ho Ho Ho says the lawman. Oh ho ho so you're the mother? Oh ho sir is she the killer? Is that so, oh? Well well what do you have to say for yourself oh? You killed him? Oh he's not dead oh? You hit him with the bottle? Ho ho ho oh don't interrupt no. I've got all I need ho ho ho come with me woman Merry Christmas sir my deepest sympathies ho ho ho! You have the right to remain silent woman don't you know? Ho ho ho! Merry Christmas!

Mummy's hands are bound and she is dragged through the hallway by the ho ho ho-ing lawman. She can't make her plea, the guardian of justice is too busy bellowing ho ho ho and she cries and daddy has more or less closed up and the lights of the ambulance and the police car outside in the night fill the room with blips of bright blue and the Christmas puppy has been silent witness to all of this until now and it all becomes too much for him so he closes his eyes in disgust and turns his face away and through the open front door he turns and gallops into the darkness with the full intention of never returning. Mummy doesn't care. Daddy doesn't care and little baby Victor certainly doesn't care. Caring is something his damaged little brain has lost the ability to ever do again.

Let's leave mummy to the lawmen for a time, they have things they have to do with her, let's go with little baby Victor and the medic and see what becomes of those two shall we? The glum medic's chest beats heavy from all the rhetoric fury he has only recently lashed screaming mummy with and through the thump-thump-thumping of his sick heart he opens the big doors to his ambulance and plonks the silent floppy baby onto a mattress within and wraps a strap around it so it doesn't flop about from the speed of the drive. Then he slams those big doors shut and gets in to drive and takes the wheel and makes the sirens whoop and howl (he likes that sound does the medic) then he drives the sad drive from the crumbling house of Christmas to the glowing white fortress of the hospital while his medic chums perform redundant pokes and pumps and pinpricks and procedures on the motionless baby Nah Mate He Aint Waking Up they prod its temple they smack its cheeks they shake its shoulders they open its eye but Nah Mate He Aint Waking Up He Aint Snuffed It Yet Though and all the while the bulleting wagon whoops and howls and there are few cars to obstruct the journey because well it's Christmas isn't it? All the owners of such things have rightly locked them in their garages and are with their families tonight well except for the medic and the lawman they have to roam the lonely streets waiting to claw damaged kid-corpses from brutal drunken women dashing their husbands' hopes of a peaceful life.

The bitches! So mumbles the medic. *Women!* So mumbles the medic. *Why do they interfere?* So mumbles the medic. *Why must they drink?* So mumbles the medic. *Why don't they know their limits anymore?* So mumbles the medic. *That sobbing daddy should have been harder on his woman if he wanted to preserve the safety of that ex-child back there.* So mumbles the medic. *He should have struck her now and then and kept her down.* So mumbles the medic. *My missus knows exactly where she belongs and my my does she ever stay there!* So mumbles the medic. *What would I do if she ever moved, what would I do?* So mumbles the man.

The ambulance arrives, the older wiser medic appears on the steps outside rubbing his arms – It's Christmas, he's cold, he'll rub his arms – and the mumbling medic snatches little baby Victor from the back of the van and brings him forth to show to his elder. He lifts the sleeping boy up by the ankles and dangles him in front of the older wiser medic who squints for a turn, shakes his head and waves the mumbling medic away dismissively – he won't even allow little baby Victor or the mumbling medic into the haven of the hospital for there isn't really any point that kid really is beyond help so back into the back of the van for little baby Victor strap him down lock those doors you chaps can call it a night if you want go and enjoy the rest of Christmas I'll be dropping this kid off at the Children's Hospice no it's alright I'll be alright on my own it's only round the corner *fucking women* have a happy one Christmas cheer have one on me and all that good will to all men of course Merry Christmas.

The mumbling medic drives on through the dark just he and little baby Victor now, hardly the most riveting company, a brain-dead baby. Like he did say the Children's Hospice is only around the corner oh but what a corner; gone instantly is the festive glow of the cul-de-sacs and the warming white light of the hospital, banished are the road signs and the shops and the well-placed little trees gone are the traffic lights and the tarmac and the pedestrian crossing and the school gate and the bus stop chocolate bar adverts and the Please Recycle bins and the errant empty crisp packets and the lampposts and the awnings and the speckles of pigeon shit and the swings and the see-saw and the cut grass and the fence and the goalposts and the benches and the roundabout and the doorbells and the net curtains and the rooftops and the driveways and the garages. What a corner – the Children's Hospice! A black-behemoth dungeon-tower atop a crumbling, spiralling mountain-top clawing up from tangled, jagged woodland on all sides, silhouetted against an impossible goliath moon and flickering from lightning bolts about its buttresses and walls and spires – and a storm of thunder and rain that the mumbling medic doesn't recall occurring in the safe but solemn land of Christmas and the Hospital batters the world now and all of his senses – and a whirling narrow road that stretches up the twisting peak is the only way to access the dreaded place and access is precisely what the lonely mumbling medic in his crawling ambulance does. He stretches out from the cramp of the confines of the car and reaches for the heavy, rusted knocker on the vast wooden door beneath the ancient engraving CHILDREN'S HOSPICE and he knocks three deep and dreadful knocks.

The door creaks open after a time and a single pale arm, open-palmed in expectation, slithers out without any more of a body to follow it from the darkness within and give humanly context to the outstretched, solitary limb.

Got one for me? It says.

Yes. Says the mumbling medic, quivering on the doorstep in the rain.

Name?

Victor.

Definitely dying?

Definitely.

Because we aint got room for kids what might get well again.

Definitely dying. We've checked.

Fine. Give it me.

And the mumbling medic passes little baby Victor to the faceless arm and the faceless arm snatches the body and both the arm and the body slink back into the darkness behind the door and the door creaks again and is closed with a resounding slam and the mumbling medic is again turned away on the doorstep and he gets back into his ambulance and drives away from the peaks and spires and storms of the barren nightmare lands and back around the corner into the peaceful Christmas evening of tarmac roads and corner shops and playgrounds and traffic lights and cul-de-sacs and his working day finally comes to its promised end and he returns to his warm home and to a loving family and if you want me to tell you that at least his life is a happy one and that he and his wife grow old never experiencing physical conflict like that of mummy and daddy and that his children reach adulthood never knowing abuse like that of little baby Victor and that his prejudices and mistrust of the fairer sex are finally suppressed by the overwhelming love and loyalty of the best woman he will ever know then fine, I'll tell you that. It is Christmas after all.

So what about mummy? Mummy is still busy with the lawmen we'll get to her yet. What about daddy? Does daddy radiate any remorse at all for his considerable part in the event? Well of course not. Does he feel it? The capability of feeling doesn't go away simply when the act does. Daddy feels. Oh how he feels. But guilt is a paralytic in action and cowardice is a motivator in silence. Daddy is silent when he needs to be and active when he needs to be too. The lawmen delicately question daddy who sinks into his sofa and clutches his face and bawls into his fingers – he's no actor he couldn't fake tears like those but those tears come from somewhere real and world be damned if daddy will ever let on where that might actually be.

She was drunk! She's always drunk! It's Christmas! The baby was already in bed! And – you might be married officer – you know how it is when you're both feeling festive and you've both had a drink – the boy was in bed – we couldn't help ourselves it was really on the spur of the moment – that fucking wine – it don't half make her frisky – we got down to it there and then – there on the carpet – this is true – your DNA boys can check her bits or something – and – I don't know – the boy must have thought we were playing or something – and – I don't know – the sight of him must have freaked her out because I was on top and I couldn't see him – so – she must have gone for him with that fucking wine bottle – 'scuse the language officer – and – I don't know – it was all a big blur – next thing I know she was screaming and the boy was down on his back – that's all I can tell you – oh God is my boy dead? Oh Lord where did they take my little boy? Oh Jesus officer! Oh Christ!

And daddy can say no more as all the true parts of his edited story flourish and fight within him and the sicknesses that they bring with them chomp at the walls of his guts and coil like smoke up his throat and flow like spilled oil into the recesses of his brain and trickle down and become tears and burst from his stinging eye sockets as the sight of all around him floods and dampens and can no longer be seen by drenched, guilty eyes.

The abstracted, submerged officer quivers closer to daddy and a wavering arm finds his back and condolences are uttered and daddy is delicately tiptoed around while he is busy with despair and he is assured that the lawmen will be in touch soon and he is sombrely invited to have a Merry Christmas if he can and he just keeps crying and the shapeless globules of men saunter out of the room and the door is closed and the sirens sound and fade and there is silence or at least there would be if daddy could manage it.

And what of mummy? Well it must be time to see how she fares with the babbling lawman and her Arthurian quest to find the elusive weapon that can break her silence against this verbally-prolapsing officer! A quest it proves to be and not one this suffering genius can manage to overcome as the lawman points his judgmental finger and saliva gushes forth from his champing stamping lips with every Ho Ho Ho and every Oh Deary Me he won't shut the gob he just keeps yelling and giggling and accusing Ho Ho Ho Oh Deary Me Oh No You Didn't You Naughty Girl Oh No Ho Ho Oh No We Got Word From Your Fella Oh No What Are You Like Oh Ho Oh No Rolling Round On That Floor Playing The Dirty Game Glugging Your Fucking Wine Oh Ho Ho Ho Aren't You A Dirty Little Show! Smacked That Baby In So You Could Carry On Oh No! Oh The Other Girls Inside Won't Take To You Much Oh No No No! They Got Kids Of Their Own They'd Kill To Hold Again And

Then They'll Meet You And Find Out What You'd Rather Do With Your Kid Just So You Can Enjoy A Quick Poke Oh No Oh Ho Ho Ho Oh No No No!

That's not how it-

OH HO HO Ho! Oh No You Don't You Don't Interrupt Oh No! You Don't Babble In This Room This Is My Room Oh Ho Ho Ho Oh Lordy Lordy Lordy Lo! Just You Keep It Closed Oh!

My husband rape-

NO NO NO NO NO NO No! Man Is Talking Little Girl So Keep It Bloody Well Closed! No No No Ho Ho Ho Keep It Bloody Well Closed!

And this is more or less how it continues to go with all the Ho Ho Ho's and the No No No's and the Keep It Closed's the babbling lawman like the mumbling medic and the thrusting daddy enforce that mummy Keep It Closed and not through a lack of trying the contrary mummy does indeed learn to Keep It Closed and for a good while too nights pass the trial rolls around sobbing daddy sits in his box silent mummy sits in hers the big justice sits in his tower and there's really little to discuss - they've got the bottle with mummy's fingerprints, they've got the baby, they've got the mumbling medic's conviction of mummy's apathy they've got poor daddy's tears and pleas they've got lawyers they've got assumptions and prejudices they've got a half-interested jury they've got room in the prison they've got mummy! They've got her! And off she goes behind slamming bars!

III

Mummy rots and cries and waits and sleeps and works and eats. She clutches the bars and she wails at the walls. She lies on her back and curls into a ball. She glares at the officer as he strolls the halls. She rejects her meals and she wobbles and falls. And so this goes, and so this goes.

And whenever she tiptoes through the corridors arms not too unlike the pale one at the Children's Hospice swipe at her and claw at her and behind them voices whoop at her and yell at her – the lawman did say it didn't he? Wronged and wrong women who have had vengeance prohibited by these big bars – these women have heard what mummy did with her boy – they don't know the truth of it the only word that gets around is the word of man – all they see is a woman who'd sooner gash up the skull of her toddler than cut short a shafting from her feller. They see a woman so detached from the expected joy of motherhood that she'd rather prowl these cold corridors eating grey gruel and draped in jumpsuits and going to sleep on hard slabs than cuddle and shush and feed her little baby. They don't know the half of it the only word that gets around is the word of man. And they promise they'll do to her what she did to little baby Victor and they don't half try. Maybe one will occasionally swipe for mummy in the shower room or the canteen. Maybe mummy's cheeks are occasionally thwacked side from side by a weaponised dinner tray – maybe mummy's ribcage is occasionally rearranged by an angry broom-handle and maybe that angry broom-handle tries to go at her again and again thwack thwack thwack and maybe it takes six or seven flustered wardens to wring it from the iron grip of the angry incarcerated mother who won't accept that there might be a little more to mummy's tale than she has been spoon-fed by hearsay. Either way, mummy's having a memorable time.

Free daddy can't visit little baby Victor, for his freedom, tenuous as it is, remains in his mind only as long as the mind is closed off to what he knows is his atrocity. Daddy's grasping justifications flick like feathers on the wind or a baby boy's balloon into the hereafter and daddy's grasp doesn't extend to accommodate their distance or make extra pains to strive to swipe them back. Look at them go, daddy. Look up at them as they float into the moonlight but Lord please don't look back down, no, even after they've been spirited away into the night Christ don't look back down for do you remember what you've left there on the ground?

And daddy looks down and there is his house he is outside it is night time the lights glow from within the shiny Christmas trinkets still wilt from the walls like rotting thieves left at the gallows and – oh, my – and – oh, dear me – and – didn't a little shadow just slink by behind the net curtain? Did daddy really see that? But nobody is inside - mummy's festering in mummy's cell, Christmas puppy ran away and little baby Victor is brain-dead on a bed in a tiny room not unlike the one he was born in but oh so harrowing that room that dark little cove sitting at the bottom of a leaking creaking corridor in the belly of a crumbling hilltop fortress leaking from the rain, flickering in the thunder the ghastly the terrible the hopeless the Children's Hospice and in its bowels the tiny, the cold, the motionless little baby strapped to machinery and without hope so far from home. So far from love. So far from Christmas. So what was behind the window daddy wonders?

Daddy shudders and walks. He lifts the collar of his coat and lowers his drenched sick head from the merciless downpour. His spirits and the powers that should know better may dance on tenterhooks but the elements hold no such grace against the damned. Daddy won't defend himself against righteous judgment, he won't clench a fist at the indictment of scowling passers-by, he won't fall to his savage knees on the free side of mummy's cage and scream sorrow and forgiveness where he knows none will be given and the only fruits of such an endeavour would be his bloodied vocal cords. But daddy will walk in the rain.

Each drop is a slicing blade gashing daddy's cheeks and shredding daddy's clothes, a crystal whip flicked from the sinewy arm of justice lashing at daddy's flesh and hacking at his quaking limbs but daddy walks on in the rain. A wasted old haggard down right dirty rotten filthy hunched little ancient wrinkled sullen scruffy stinking bastard stands on the horizon, head cocked to the side like a curious dog as daddy approaches and daddy – drunk on remorse – spies some respite from his Earthly accuser in this torrential passion play. Old Tramp! shouts daddy. Old Tramp no don't scarper old mate please stay there old tramp come over here put down that rotten cloth and come here no I'm not going to rob you no I will not fight you just come here you shrivelled little affront to society for the love of God come here! And the old tramp does what daddy says for daddy is the society that has shunned him and old tramp the ousted Adam wants his scowling maker to give him back some warmth, to let him back into the Garden for fuck's sake! But daddy scowls on ever ashamed even as the open-armed old tramp approaches to await further instruction.

Look at this tenner old tramp! Yes it's real. You can have it.

And the old tramp animates and swipes for the crumpled, promised tenner but daddy hoists it out of reach with a Now Now and a Tut Tut and a Not So Fast old tramp you can have it I said but first I'd like you to lay into me. Strike me, bite me, kick me, kick all manner of shit out of me. I won't fight back. I won't fight back. I won't have you carted off by the cunts in charge. Just hurt me. Attack me. Make me bleed. Do whatever you want to me. I won't scream and I won't run I'll just stagger back to my empty home and you will be ten pounds the better man than you are now and you can buy whatever scumbags like you long to buy with your unearned pickings.

I'm an old man.

I said I won't fight back.

I'm not violent.

Even for a reward?

I've never hit someone before.

I don't believe you. Hurt me. Punch, kick, slap, scratch, nut, chin, crack, gash, shaft me you ugly little toad! Daddy thumps his chest with two fists in his roaring plea. Do it! Do it! Hurt me! DO IT!

Old tramp gasps and recoils but daddy means business and old tramp could use the money so old tramp finds his beast the one that should be raging against the dying light of compassion but will have to be satiated simply baying at the shrieking frame of this fat angry man so old tramp bellows and leaps and swipes at daddy and punches his cheeks and scratches his flesh and throttles his throat and thuds his fat gut and bites his big ears and spits blood at the murderer's face and strikes it left right left right and daddy's right he doesn't scream he doesn't run he doesn't defend so old tramp kicks daddy and shoves him to the concrete and stomps on the belly and bursts the shirt and footprints of blood and mud compile as the stomps keep coming and old tramp a werewolf now never the frail, decrepit runt of the world's litter is descending on daddy and rising with blood flowing from his jaws and shredded flesh lodged in his muddied fingernails and daddy quivers like the mangled Christmas bird on the ground and old tramp shrieks and howls and stomps and gouges and bites and rips and chews and head-butts the silent, mangled daddy until he can attack no more for this exertion of rage is not familiar to him and fatigue has cut it short as fatigue is wont to do.

Gasping, bleeding, snorting and streaming daddy shakily finds his feet and stands – a heaving hulk of blood and filth and torn garments staring exhaustedly at his violent slave. Meagre old tramp steps back worriedly and holds out his hand for his reward. Daddy grins a glistening red grin of blood-stained broken teeth and flicks old tramp's winnings at the floor. There is some peace here now for daddy who watches old tramp scrabble to his knees and chase the tenner as it wafts to the ground.

Good says daddy Good old tramp you really did yourself proud there and here you go have your prize buy some fucking wine or a shuffle with a slut or whatever the hell that crumpled piece of shrapnel will get you and one more thing I said I promised didn't I promise I said I wouldn't fight back didn't I say that? (and the old tramp nods) and I didn't fight back did I? (and the old tramp shakes his head) but the fight is over and I never said I wouldn't do this.

And daddy does what he never said he wouldn't do he's still an angry hungry man and he takes the old tramp and before the old tramp knows what's hit him, daddy hits him. He takes old tramp's bird neck in both hands and he squeezes and old tramp can't scream but then in all fairness daddy didn't scream and daddy squeezes and roars and crushes whatever is inside that old neck and old tramp's eyes roll back and his breath goes out and his head falls limp and daddy still squeezes just to make sure and when he is sure he lets go and watches old tramp's corpse slump to the wet concrete and daddy's glare remains on the old dead tramp.

You Can Keep The Tenner says daddy. You're A Better Man Now. And daddy keeps walking. Heavens, nobody saw that? Not to worry, he's going home. He's got some making up to do. Home is where the heart is and the only heart that still beats in this dreaded affair is poor mummy's heart while Victor is sleeping and daddy is throttling tramps why is poor mummy's heart still beating? Daddy walks to the only home he deserves and he throws open the doors and he sees the man at his little desk and he treads blood and rainwater into the lounge and he bleeds from the head and he bleeds from the gums and he bleeds from the gut and he bleeds from the neck and he bleeds from the eye and he bleeds from the heart (which is dead) and he looks at the startled officer and he says;

My name is Victor. My wife is innocent. I've just killed a tramp *and* I killed my son.

I know you! I was at your house! Your son isn't dead!
You know that he soon will be.
True. Why did you kill your son?
He got in the way. I was raping my wife.
Why did you rape your wife?
She angered me.
Why did you kill the tramp?
To prove that I'm a killer. The world thinks my wife did it.
Why would you want to prove that you're a killer?
Because I need to suffer for my crime.
Aren't you suffering already?
A bit.
Where is the tramp now?
Outside in the rain.
Do you want me to arrest you?
Yes.

That's very noble of you.

It is not noble. I just know where I belong.

Your wife would be freed.

So she should be.

You threw the bottle then?

No, my wife did.

Then she is the killer.

She was trying to fend me off. It is my fault.

You said before that it was all a blur.

I was a liar then.

You're not one now?

I kept my word to the tramp. I'm confessing to this. I'm not a liar anymore. But I'm still a killer.

What was your word to the tramp?

That I wouldn't fight him.

You killed him.

But I didn't *fight* him. That I would pay him.

You killed him.

But I still *paid* him. That I wouldn't rob him.

You killed him.

But I didn't *rob* him.

You killed him.

But I didn't rob him.

Yes you did. You robbed him of all he had. You took his life. You are a liar yet.

I suppose I am. Then arrest me all the quicker please.

Certainly. I am arresting you for the murders of your son and the homeless man and for the rape of your wife on Christmas day. You do not have to say anything, but it may harm your defence if you do not mention when questioned something which you may later rely on in court. Anything you say may be given in evidence.

Then I'll say again that I raped my wife, killed my son and killed the tramp and have it over with as quickly as possible.

And it is most certainly quick. The lawmen and the justices furrow their brows in smoky lounges and speak of the crime and the new light that has been shone upon it and they think of suffering mummy being badgered in the clink and they say Whoopsie Daisies and they shrug and bite their lips and the yawning judge saunters back to his highchair in the courthouse and mummy and daddy are each ushered in – daddy bruised and dead-eyed mummy frail and pale and quivering – there isn't much of a reunion to speak of for their relationship has soured somewhat in recent weeks – and the men bite their knuckles in embarrassment and say Terribly Sorry Missus and they give her shackles to daddy and boot his bottom into the meat wagon and an apologetic handshake is offered to mummy but she doesn't fancy reciprocating just now she just wants to be home and be with her – oh, no – she just wants to be home, but home is where the heart is and where the bloody hell can that be now?

Well anyway mummy is dropped onto her doorstep (it is hers that home it always was hers not daddy's – her melodies paid for that doorstep and all that lies beyond it) and now she is back in the heartless home and there's the sofa and the television that made daddy so angry on Christmas day and there's the piano stool that little baby Victor used to love so much and there's the piano that paid for the home and tipped daddy to breaking point and there's the Christmas tree still not packed away (mummy's sure that's bad luck) and Christmas puppy's water bowl still filled but with no Christmas puppy to lap from it and to be honest it's all a bit much for poor tormented mummy who's been the frail, protesting punch bag for angry men and angry women for weeks and weeks now and here she is back in the heartless home and with all its creature comforts and mod-cons and familiarity it is the worst place she has been in yet. Mummy raises her shivering hands to her dripping eyes at the empty sight of it all and she lets go. There is no broom-wielding inmate to descend upon her for drawing attention to herself this time; mummy can cry and wail as loud and as long and she likes and she very well shall do.

Bedtime comes shortly after. Mummy is dried out and weather-beaten from the crying and closing the eyes proves to be a real stinger so for the time being she keeps them open – it's dark anyway so it makes little difference – and there's just far too much to think about to allow for sleep to come any time soon. Fat daddy's dent lies beside her upon the mattress and there's an errant pair of briefs over there somewhere too. No doubt encrusted with skid marks. Sleep eludes mummy. The bedroom is silent. Silent and dark. But sleep eludes mummy. Slithers of moonlight in place of the complete absence of light lend distorting blue-grey shadow to all of the items around her. A tower of darkness behind the moderately-sized lamp. A colossal, bulbous mound behind the dresser stool. Little things have big effects in the over-aware state of mind that the witching hour brings to the sleepless. That disturbance – whatever it is – sounds like the pattering of tiny little feet making their way closer to the bedside. Whether or not that's the boiler or the sink in the next room – it sounds like faint, gurgling laughter gradually getting louder with proximity. Is that an itch on mummy's face? A twiddling fiddle with the tip of her nose – a poke in the eye! Eurgh! A spider! No – too big to be a spider – a little hand – not him – no – he's not dead – he can't be a ghost – but what else can it be? He pats and pokes mummy's face in the darkness like he used to and he giggles like he used to too – and mummy splutters and winces and her chest pounds and he's there! A little round head – blue either of flesh or in the moonlight – big eye sockets absent of eyes – a slimy wide smile loosened by dribble giggles and little hands patter up and down, slapping mummy's cheeks and he smiles down above her and then those little hands try to open mummy's jaw and climb into her gob but mummy cries out and sits up and can't take another second in this wretched house why is my baby boy a ghost now? Has he already left me so soon? I must go to the Children's Hospice! I must go there at once! And mummy leaps from the suddenly Victor-less bed and dresses and runs far away from the heartless home and makes her way to the storm-bound towers of that dreaded place where her poor baby boy lies still – be he dead, be he alive. Please be alive. Please be alive. Please please please please please.

As always is the case, the surfeit of pedestrian paraphernalia melts away as mummy's taxi turns the corner into the jagged, howling world of the Children's Hospice. The driver – bestowed with mummy's tearful urgency – screeches his vehicle to a halt before the lofty old doors beneath the stone engraving CHILDREN'S HOSPICE and mummy thanks and pays and emerges into the pistol-shot rainstorm and pounds desperately on the splintering wood and before long the door creaks open and that pale arm slides out.

Dropping one off or visiting?
Visiting!
Name?
His? Victor.
Come in.

The giant door swings further open with a guttural creak and before mummy stands a young, crooked man who smiles formally, ushers her into the dripping darkness, begins speaking and never ever shuts his gob again.

IV

Oh yeah yeah you're the mummy aint you the mummy? Well yeah yeah step in out the storm mummy come it's bloody dreadful out there we don't boast the most warming of shelters here at the Children's Hospice but for the love of Him up there we do try our best for the sick little littl'uns.

My name is Skippins I'm the nurse man here at the Children's Hospice yeah yeah some say I aint a real man but what are they who have to bellow that claim? Christ Almighty can we shuffle like worm-ridden dogs on their itchy arseholes out of this stifling, backward tide of prejudice yet? Heavens above must men prove the worth of their sex by denying the right of it to others who simply want to get by? Yeah yeah follow me this way mummy it's Victor you came for aint it? You're the one who conked your boy with a bottle aint you? Yeah yeah they told me all. Your fella raped you didn't he?

Yeah yeah well stressful times like Christmas are when pricks prove their worth and he sounds like a prick – oh no your boy wasn't – er – isn't newborn is he? He was –er – is – two, wasn't – er – isn't he? Yeah yeah well follow me missus don't mind the pipes they leak and leak and we can't seem to do much about that just step around them. And don't mind the lights they flicker and pop and we can't do much about that either yeah yeah this is an old shell of a wretched fortress the hospital down the road – I suppose your kid was born there – they have all the funding, their pipes run like portals to Heaven their lights beam like the smiles of Angels but here we are dodging drip drops and feeling walls in the dark we don't get much aint no sense for them in charge to pump money into the upkeep of litt'luns who are about to snuff it either way. Snuff it in dark or snuff it in light what difference does it make? When you're dead you're dead and it's dark and damp there anyway mark my words missus I know this.

Yeah yeah I'm sort of the last salvation in these litt'luns fleeting lives I guess I'm their guardian angel, I don't know, I don't want to put myself on the Holy pantheon but well I roam these corridors day and night and with the lack of window and the flickering lamps I barely know what's day or what's night anymore but I have a job to do. I'm appointed to keep these kids in – well – hope aint really the word, most of 'em – the ones what can still think anyway so not your Victor – most of 'em know they aint long for this life, we tell them that when they come in to keep them in check. Hope is like sugar to a baby boy, give him too much and he'll climb the bloody walls and I got enough work to do without being a huffy bloody playmate as well. That's why we feed them the fish mush. That fishy gruel keeps 'em down. They suck that oily fish mush up and they're fed but they aint too nourished. Keeps the damn kids down that fish mush. I carry the fish mush and spoon it out to them. Four spoons of fish mush a day. Then they burp and fart and in all honesty these corridors more or less always smell like fish mush and I suppose I more or less always smell like fish mush too – I can't be sure – I never really leave this cavern – but I think I smell like fish mush – oh as it happens that's the kitchen where the fish mush is made. Simons the cook he makes the fish mush all day and all night he pounds them fishes with a mallet made of wood he pounds and pounds I don't think he even knows he's doing it anymore we pay him a humble wage but he just stays here and pounds and pounds the dead fishes and scoops the fishy paste into a pot and I take the pot of fish mush and a little ladle and I feed the fish mush to the kids and Simons keeps on pounding the fishes can you hear? Bang bang bang that's Simons alright, pounding the fishes into fish mush. And with the bits he don't use he hurls them out the windows and Lance the strange boy that lurks in the alleys outside the Children's Hospice, he eats the leftovers he don't half love the fish does Lance. Like the kids in here, it's all he ever eats. Lance just prowls the alleys waiting for them fish bits to come pouring out of the kitchen window and he reaches into the bins to grab the fish bits and he gnaws at them all night. Good source of omega three. You might have the privilege of meeting strange Lance later on – he's skinny like a snake and oily like a fish, you won't miss him. I'll come back for the fish mush later when you're seeing your boy.

But yeah yeah I'm all these kids have, most of their mummies and daddies don't bother popping by – I wonder why you did missus to be honest you know your boy is braindead don't you? – well yeah yeah alright – they don't bother popping by because what difference does it make? Well they don't know Heaven is cold and wet and they don't know it's because Jesus aint home and if they did they'd all defecate and crawl to their kids with streaming tears lubricating the journey and sliding them here on their slippery knees in no time but they don't know and Christ Above if it's my job to let them know that my bosses aint told me.

Yeah yeah I'm not full of myself, I know these kids see me as a Father figure, a good Angel sent to usher them into a sound sleep, I ain't a selfish person, I ain't a selfish man, I know the plight of the lonely as much as I know the plight of the clan and I'm just Skippins I'm just a man here to do a job and change what little of life is left for these kids. Keep up missus! Your baby boy's cell is right at the bottom of this corridor and it winds and it slopes and there are puddles so keep that in mind – feel the walls if you want – hold my shoulders if you must oh yeah yeah and ignore the doors for some of them have eyes and they'll look into yours and without hearing a word you'll hear them scream Save Me and without knowing why you might just be compelled to scuttle over and rattle the bolted door and scream I Will Save You, God knows I've seen weaker-willed women do just that, I don't know you from Adam you might be strong – though you would have conked your man successfully with that wine bottle if you were, I don't know maybe you were drunk it might not be your fault you've probably turned that over in your head once or twice so I shan't linger on that – but don't look at the doors or the eyes because we've got somewhere to be anyway you will have noticed that I'm a pleasing chap – you don't find angels who aint – yeah yeah they chose me to inhabit these chambers because the little dying kids would want to see beauty before the end – well they'll die never having really grasped the concept of it because who can unless they've seen enough of the other thing? Sure some of these kids have already had a fair old bit of strife in their short turns on Earth – been made to grow up faster if you will – but they are still kids and what they really want to do is eat and dribble and cry like all selfish babies – *Back in your bed, Horace* – so does beauty have any more worth to them than a Kinder Egg or an

Action Man? When they go to the cold, wet Heaven they might just continue to grow and they'll need a concept of beauty if they want to do just that and that, missus, is where I come in.

We got all sorts here. All manner of dying kids brain-dead or just sick in the guts where no Earthly medicine will shoo the parasites in them. Look at Cindy – that thing in her neck keeps her breathing but personally I don't see why, there aint nothing we can do. Tell you what missus, go and try and open Cindy's door, see what happens. Go on don't be shy-

Haha! You see? Cindy's mummy and daddy's house had a bad spirit in it. They'd have to turn in quite early because when the moon came up the house would go bad and the spirit would waft through the lower levels breaking things – they spent a killing on plates they did – and slamming doors and pounding walls and screeching and wailing – they learned to be strong sleepers they did – and this would happen every night and they never dared set foot on those lower levels but Cindy had the foolish intrepidness of all kids – they hadn't gotten round to scaring that out of her even with that rackety spirit whirling about the place nightly – and she just wanted a cold glass of milk and she weren't sleepy and she weren't scared and she waltzed into that kitchen calm as you like and before she could even say Semi-Skimmed she was lifted into the air and slammed into the ceiling with the force of a vacuum. They did warn her. Every bone broken and brain shut down but Lord will she ever die? God knows! Well Cindy's parents don't have that spirit any more and now they drink and dance into the tiny hours at their own leisure without disturbance because that spirit came here with Cindy and go near her cell and the whole Hospice shakes like it did when you touched the door – sorry to startle you haha but see what I mean?

Then there's this little boy Alex you'd think he was an alabaster sculpture wouldn't you for all he moves or blinks or for the colour in his cheeks Of Which There Is None. He can't have long left – you can look in his eyes don't worry he won't know you're there – look at him, upright and startled and in that very pose when he was carted here four months back – he had a bad dream and walked in on his mummy and daddy hunched on all eights doing the *wrong* sex – you know the one I mean – and he turned white from head to toe in half a second with a reaction so vivid it was as if he'd suffered more than a mere witness – and he could never sit down or blink again. He's only a wee lad, he'll collapse soon enough.

I know it's getting too dark to see but keep walking missus – there'll be sporadic bursts of fluorescent light to help you see your way besides – and hold my shoulders if you will – some of the eyes have lights in too but keep them in your periphery or you know what will happen I just told you oh but hang about you have to see this one you won't believe – hold tight let me just light the cell – ta da! – now I'll prod him with this pole and he should wake – there you go – see how Ralph scuttles about his cell like an arachnid – you ever seen a kid able to do that? See how fast he is on his crooked hands and knees – see Ralph scuttle to the right, now to the left, now backwards, look how his head is cocked at that inhuman angle – it aint right is it? Haha he's a human spider – one of the wardens reckons he saw him scuttling up the wall once though I aint never seen that – oi Ralph – hang on I'll poke again – haha there he goes! Off into the corner just like a real aggravated spider! Do you want to know why? Ralph was taken on holiday to a country I can't bloody well pronounce and he was taken into the desert for a day trip and when his parents weren't looking a great big creature the exact size of Ralph – with plenty of hairy legs and pincers and fiery red eyes – scuttled out of the sand and forced itself into Ralph's open mouth – Ralph was screaming at the time you see so that made it easy for the creature – it wriggled down Ralph's throat and with its legs and bulk it filled Ralph up and now Ralph is of the shape and agility of the very creature within. I tell you what I'd love to know the full story of how the hell they got him back home – but we ain't even sure if Ralph is still in there or if the creature has completely consumed his insides and is just using his stretchy flesh as a fitted jacket – we're all too squeamish and jumpy to check but it don't matter too much because the parents sure as Hell don't want him back. Alright Ralph back in your bed now it's time to sleep or whatever it is you do when those red eyes close and those limbs coil up over your torso.

Nearly there missus. We've come to the lowest level of the Hospice now. Lord it aint half wet down here. Are you crying? Your boy's cell is at the end of this corridor I know it's more or less completely pitch black now but you aint going to trip over a kid or nothing – that has happened to visitors before but we're a bit more thorough these days – oh did I remember to lock Ralph's cage? Anyway you see that door at the end – that is your Victor's door it ain't locked you can go first and see him and say what you need to say if you need to say anything. Let it be said missus that there's a lot on the other side of this door so *don't* let it be said I'm one for blathering on and on needlessly, I'll say no more and step to one side and in you go missus.

Skippins steps aside and mummy stops. In the near-complete absence of light she can dimly make out his lopsided frame in the corner of her eye and the silvery streak of light ahead signals the little metal door behind which lies her child. She places shaking fingers on the metal handle and her other palm on the smooth, cold, grey door and she twists the handle and she pushes the door and there is a thin squeak as she makes the delicate push and passes wraith-like into the tiny room which is as dark as the spiralling corridors behind her save for a low spotlight which beams a murky glow down onto the slab beneath it. And on that slab? It is him. Little baby Victor – as still and as tiny as on that dreadful Christmas day – stretched out on his back – naked save for damp, shrivelled diaper – eyes closed as ever – tiny fingers curled upwards (toes too) – some twisted tubes clasped around his face and arms – coiling out to the left and linking the little boy to a burly mechanical box of some kind which beeps occasionally and whirs intermittently – it is keeping the baby alive, supposes mummy. She tiptoes further into the room and approaches little baby Victor whose inanimate features gain greater clarity the closer she gets and when she is close enough mummy places a soft hand on her baby boy's chest and out come the tears.

Why did he haunt me tonight?

Excuse me missus?

He came to me earlier. When I was in bed. A ghost.

I fancy you gotta be dead to be a ghost.

Then is he dead?

Don't fink so.

So how could he haunt me?

His brain is dead.

So?

Well the mind is all there is, innit? If the brain is dead then the king is dead. The mind rules the body and the mind – the king – is dead. Your boy has gotten free of his body, I fancy. Lives on a different plane now, I fancy. God knows. I don't get paid to philosophise I'm just here to feed him his fish mush. Though this one can't even swallow it and the others are probably getting hungry now. You can hear all their bellies rumbling up the corridors it's right gross. You say what you need to say I've gotta go see Simons for the fish mush.

Skippins leaves the room and slams the door behind him and his incongruously jolly whistle echoes and fades into the long corridors behind him. It doesn't cross his mind that mummy might not be able to find her way back through the crooked labyrinth in the dark without him for his mind is solely on his fishy task. Mummy doesn't particularly care at this point – she never wants to leave her baby's side and poor little baby Victor just lies there as motionless as the slab beneath him and the murky light above.

I'm sorry my baby.

No response.

Mummy and daddy both love you (she's making an assumption on daddy's behalf of course).

Nothing.

We never meant to hurt you. We never wanted anything besides all the happiness and joy and comfort in the universe for you. For you to remain tucked into a blanket of our undying love forever. For you to exist purely in a world of promises and dreams under a loving moon and a warming sun. For you, our Christmas joy, to keep Christmas in your heart all your long life and to take with you all the good things we could possibly give you into your adventure where you can have your own little babies and give them all the love and promise you can. There were to be brothers and sisters for you to play with – daddy and I used to dream about seeing you teaching your baby sister all the things you've learned – Amelia would have been her name – and you would have shared your toys and she would have learned to say your name and whenever you were parted each of you would have smiled and laughed at the mention of reunion and as the years went by we'd all sit around the Christmas table together under the Christmas tree and your sons and daughters and nieces and nephews – mine and daddy's grandchildren – would all be there and they'd play on the carpet like you and Amelia used to when you were just babies and your wife or husband would be like another daughter or son to us and we'll go on holidays together and laugh and drink in the warmth of an exotic sunset. And I'll help you with your wedding plans and I'll teach your sister piano so she can play at the ceremony like she always hoped to and I'll pay for the deposit on your first house and furnish it if you need – not that you need to because you have a very good job Victor I'm so proud of you, how far you've come since you were that little baby boy on my knee giggling and clapping as I played piano – you're so clever and you look just like your daddy.   Happy birthday Victor don't get too drunk will you! Amelia's coming round in the afternoon, with her kids. We'll have a lovely birthday-slash-Christmas just like we always do. No doubt daddy will be asleep on the settee by half past four. We'll put his Christmas CD on and you can sing merrily along to SHAKIN' STEVENS just like you always do. And Amelia will laugh her head off as ever. On Boxing Day shall we go and visit nan? Or we can wait till the day after if your kids need a bit of a rest – they get really hyper after all that excitement don't they? But then they take after their dad and you used to be the same, well swap chocolate for brandy and I suppose you haven't changed too much. That's for having your birthday on Christmas day I suppose, two celebrations rolled into one! But I wish you wouldn't drink so much Victor, it can't be good for your liver. Yes I know I had a bit of a drinking problem when I was younger but I haven't touched that fucking wine in years now, not since you were a baby. Maybe I'm to blame for all of this. Must be hereditary. What do your kids think when they see you in that state? What if you do something silly like leave the hob on overnight and then something dreadful happens? I know it's a horrible thing to say but it is a concern of mine! Do you know how many kids suffer because of drunken parents? Don't you dare call me that! I just want what's best for you! You're not listening! You're ungrateful, you've always been ungrateful! Do what you want then! Drink yourself to death and take those poor kids with you in the process. You're a waste of space like your father and I'll bet you end up in a cage just like he did! I wish I never had you!

As mummy screams and cries she doesn't notice that Skippins has returned to the room. With raised eyebrows and a bit lip he listens to mummy's rant.

Alright there missus?

Mummy spins around and roars. Men don't let me speak! I'm a genius! I've been shoved and dragged around by men since this fucking ordeal started and I refuse to let them do that to me anymore! Beaten and raped, condemned by angry medics, spat at by babbling policemen, dragged to jail by fat judges, ignored by wardens and led through this dank hell by a crooked egomaniac who won't shut up! I'm a genius and men won't let me speak!

Prove you're a genius.

Why should I prove myself to men?

Prove it to Victor.

What does he matter? He's brain-dead.

His brain is dead but as we've established, his mind ain't. Whether the body is theoretically dead or actually dead (and at this he pokes the baby with his index finger) – oh, whoops, turns out it is actually dead after all. Must have happened while you were screaming at it – anyway, it doesn't really matter.

My boy is dead?

It doesn't really matter – he weren't getting any more alive was he? All children die – even the lucky ones. Prove to Victor that you're a genius. Don't prove it to your husband, or the medic, or the policeman, or the judges, or the wardens, or me – quite rude of you to call me a crooked egomaniac by the by but I've been called worse – prove it to him. His mind still lives. He is free now.

This is all rather too much for mummy and in floods of tears at the news of little baby Victor's bodily demise she clasps at her face and issues a scream that turns Skippins' stomach – no mean feat given his day job – and in hasty expectation he shifts to one side and as he swiftly predicted mummy bolts for the door and glides with the speed of a sparrow through the corridors, still screaming and crying of course. The way back comes naturally to her despite the twists and the turns and the darkness and the identical doors and the parades of dead-eyed children glaring from the window panes of those doors and the fact that she has her face in her hands. Mummy darts up from the depths of the Children's Hospice all the way up and up until she finds herself at that imposing wooden door which she slams effortlessly open and passes through into the unyielding downpour in the night outside. She howls in misery at the raining sky but her cries are mostly lost in the cackling thunder. A skinny slimy boy crawls on his hands and knees from a shady lane beside the Hospice to see what all the fuss is about. A gnawed, dead trout dangles from his teeth and his eyes light up in wonder and shock at mummy's despondent howling. But he is mostly interested in all the oily fish corpses piled up in his alley waiting for him so he quickly creeps back to his midnight feast and leaves mummy be. Till the next time, Lance.

Mummy makes her way home on foot. She takes the descending stone path from the Children's Hospice and gathers momentum from the downward flight – she nearly trips time and again and she moves too fast for her own good and there is the possibility that the mounting speed will not allow her to stop and that she would bullet all the way home, only then severing the movement with a painful face-first slap against the front door. She is at the foot of the incline now and she swoops into the wet woods and past the petrified trees tramping on twigs and stones and animal shit along the way as wild white eyes follow her from the pitch-black thicket all around. Lightning assists her on the way and thunder claps and rumbles all around – shaking the trees and scattering the eyes – and obviously mummy doesn't slow down for she still has all that residual kinetic motivation from the steep sprint. She is drenched through and through but her concern for the dampness is barely skin-deep and finally she emerges from the wild forest and turns a corner and there is no longer thunder or rain or crumbling mountains or gargantuan moons or crooked spires, instead there are straight tarmac roads and mown lawns and distant car horns and benches and bins and kerbs and gravel and Londis and this passes by in a seemingly endless, unchanging cycle until mummy zooms into her door which doesn't curtail her motion for she left it open which was rather silly of her really but her mind was elsewhere at the time. And through the hallway she goes and head-first into the Christmas tree which wobbles as she stops and falls over taking the television with it and mummy finds the settee and down she goes onto it and into the cushion she pushes her face and screams a muffled scream which the neighbours might hear because she still hasn't gotten around to shutting the front door.

V

Little baby Victor is dead. He'll never crawl or toddle or walk or run or fly. He'll never grow to learn of love and he'll never feel the warmth of a tender cuddle or a motherly lullaby. He'll never outgrow his little dungarees or move from cot to bed or donate his baby teeth to that fairy or go to big school or make new friends or start noticing pretty girls or move into his own place. He's a tiny little cold corpse on an even colder slab and he'll be put under the ground soon where time will take his flesh away and crumble his baby bones.

But no. Victor will still grow. Freed from the body forced upon him by mummy and daddy is a consciousness that isn't going anywhere and why should it? Victor continues to thrive there. Why else would he have visited mummy that night?

These things carousel round and around in mummy's mind as she rocks on her side upon the comfy settee. Her screams fatigue her and become snivels. Her snivels become whimpers and her whimpers become heavy breaths and then silence. The traditionally elusive sleep finally finds mummy but with renewed energy on subsequent mornings screaming seems of little use so her outpour of anguish crescendos with whimpering. Whimpering in bed, whimpering in the bathroom, whimpering at the breakfast table beside the superfluous cereal bowl (she's not hungry), whimpering on the settee, whimpering on the toilet, whimpering round and round and all the day long and all the way back up to bed.

One night comes not too dissimilar to that which drove mummy out of bed and into the Children's Hospice. Just as she feels ready to drop off and dream she hears a slow tapping about the corner of her bedroom. Tap tap tap it goes like little footsteps but not as light as before – they sound slightly bigger this time and like last time they grow ever so slightly louder as they approach – slowly now. Tap. Tap. Tap. Here he comes again through the dark it's little baby Victor it must be. He's bigger now and the oblique silhouette of his bulbous bald head arrives at mummy's bedside and mummy's eyes are wide and she may see what little she may see. A high-toned voice whispers *Mummy* and – Victor has said his first word! And at that the low head begins to rise up and up from behind the bedside his hollow eye-sockets ascend into view and his sickly grin follows soon after and

Victor continues to grow and he stands upright beside the bed now looking black-eyed down at mummy and getting ever bigger a great big bald baby and he says *Mummy* again and he stretches out a desiring little hand which also seems to inflate with the rest of him and mummy's eyes are closing – she is frightened but still tired – and as that growing hand gets closer and closer to mummy's face everything falls to shadow and all is lost and the next thing that touches mummy is the break of day.

And what a day. Funeral day. Mummy can scarcely believe she has already whimpered and rocked her way through the temporal void that is the time between a death and a funeral but here it comes now. It is all misery – in fact it is chilly misery for it is well and truly January now and therefore already the very worst time of the year and one which we all bafflingly herald the arrival of with merriment and midnight kisses. Why do we do that while we let summer simply sneak up on us? Aren't we a load of silly old broken biscuits? Well January is miserable enough without the addition of a dead baby but be that as it may mummy has just that to pile onto this four-week Christmas hangover. Funeral day in January – chilly misery dead baby funeral day in January – could there possibly be anything worse in all the world?

Daddy can't come to Victor's burial for he is not allowed out at all. Can't have baby-slaughtering-festive-rapists running amok about town unattended so daddy (who has been glumly informed of Victor's passing by a nominated warden already) buries his guilty face in his naughty hands as he perches motionless on the slab of a bed and he roars woe immeasurable and even the big lads who've elected daddy as their plaything (because what else does a baby-killing rapist deserve?) even they keep schtum as they see and hear this in fact the whole wing of the prison goes silent as it sees and hears this and though the big lads will resume their lusty pastime soon enough you'd never believe it at this very moment. And what of the old tramp whom daddy robbed of life? Who came to his funeral? The councilman was there and *maybe* God but that's it – the councilman's duty to oversee as the old tramp's bones were shoved into a little hole in a pauper's boneyard amidst untrimmed weeds and crooked crosses and where no one ever comes to visit and if you think the Children's Hospice is a sorry place then go and spend an afternoon in the pauper's boneyard I dare you.

Anyway we were talking about mummy were we not? Can we please get back to mummy? Is that okay with you? Good. So mummy saunters over to the funeral and so she must and it is a lonely affair – two years on God's Earth afforded little time for Victor to make friends you see and Amelia never actually managed to get conceived despite mummy's imaginative exaggeration earlier in the week beside Victor's deathbed. So without friends or a sister or a daddy there's only mummy and the priest and even the priest barely knew the lad. The priest reiterates how Man That Is Born Of Woman Hath But A Short Time On Earth (and doesn't mummy know it?) and says Man again and again even though Victor never was and never will be a man and in the churchyard the mean January air nips at mummy's skin and frosts her tearful eyes so she blinks and rubs her arms and sits alone as steamy ghosts flourish from her lips and little baby Victor's shoebox sized coffin is plonked down into the little hole prepared earlier that day. And the priest drones on and mummy rubs her arms and in the furthest corner of her eye she notices a little hairball rollicking somewhat by the cemetery gate and she is rather concerned with Victor's farewell shindig to really bother looking around but it don't half seem familiar. Of course it is it's the one she forgot all about throughout this adventure it's almost certainly Christmas puppy making an appearance to say goodbye to his smiling little buddy Victor. Didn't daddy say that dog would watch one of them go under? Well it has been established that daddy is a man of his word and there's Christmas puppy wagging mournfully as Victor's box goes under the ground and keeping a sorry eye on cold suffering mummy who should really try and restrict her outdoor sit-downs to the summer months from here on out. He keeps a vigil by the gate and slinks backwards into shadow before mummy can turn for a proper look and confirm that it really is Christmas puppy (although between you and I, it is).

And there we have it. Little baby Victor is under the ground and the party is over and the priest has gone home and mummy remains in the graveyard in the horrible January cold (January!) and looks at the as-of-yet unmarked patch of earth beneath which lies her little baby boy and she can't have it she can't leave him in there he's her pride and joy not a pack of seeds. She's a genius and she must figure out a way to have him with her always she must figure it out she never planned for Victor's destiny to be an eternity of spouting fungus in the shade of mossy stone and trite condolences. Victor may not be coming back to mummy but maybe his body can come back with her who says it has to be buried or burned to ash why can't it stay at home where it belongs with mummy? At least give her that. He will never fall asleep at her soft songs or clap his hands as he learns to read simple words he'll never get to holding the dinner spoon all by his little self or remembering by heart the shoelace-tying rhyme no no none of that but he can still physically be with mummy yes? Above all else at least give her that.

So mummy wracks her brain and suffers and cries and screams for days and looks to every outlet for an idea and stuffing comes to mind (no we mustn't remove his insides we've already taken enough from him) and freezing comes to mind (no he is no more a fish finger than he is a pack of seeds) and an urn on the mantel (NO!) and all of these possibilities flit this way and that in mummy's screaming genius brain but none of them satisfy and then her quest delves into more obscure methods – the clock is ticking, the gravedigger won't exhume a corpse too rotten – and at last mummy comes to one that piques her addled interest! It seems that nowadays one may inter a dead loved one into a specially-crafted piece of furniture that preserves the remains and lets out no odours of decomposition – granddad in the pool table, grandma in the bookcase, uncle in the wardrobe and so forth. This sounds golden to mummy. Where should she put little baby Victor? Why of course! Little baby Victor loved so much to sit on that blessed piano stool while mummy made melodies – he'd clap his hands and try to join in and giggle and bop on his bottom like he were Mozart's fiery protégé – where else? It's the perfect size too! So mummy contacts the specialist-corpse-memorial-furniture people and requests that her little boy be dug up and his coffin cranked open and his stiff body dropped into that stool so she can be with him for all time – he'll be right where he always loved to be after all oh little baby Victor aren't you a lucky little boy? Aren't you a special little boy? Aren't you a clever little boy? Well what else could you be with a genius for a mother? And as mummy so wishes Victor's corpse is hoisted up from the dirt, toppled out of the little coffin and delivered to the furniture men who adapt and reinforce mummy's piano stool (good as new!) and deliver it back to her with little baby Victor sound asleep inside. And henceforth mummy sits on the stool and thus on her dead boy too and plays lilting laments and sad sonatas and chilling concertos while little baby Victor lies beneath her. She awakes at dawn and rushes to the piano and plays on and on the longest, saddest sounds but the most beautiful a broken genius could ever conceive and she plays them all the long day until the sun goes away and she can play no more and then she sleeps and does it all again and all the while by her side – beneath her buttocks – there is her loyal loving little baby boy her joy her companion her accomplice in the compositions and this continues day in day out day in day out until something breaks within mummy as sudden and as slant as her finished fingers dropping tunelessly onto the keys for the final time. It is not enough! He is not really here! I freed his mind from his body and I thought that the body would be ample companionship but it is not so! I need him proper! Where can I find him?

Slipping awkwardly from the overused piano and in such floods of tears that breathing proves a challenge mummy flops to the carpet and with screw-faced blindness shakes and punches the stool beside her which has Victor inside it. She pounds the leather and shakes it by the legs and cries Oh My Boy and Victor can be heard bumping and rolling around inside as she aggravates her musical seat Where Are You Victor? Where Are You? Come Back To Me!

You know where I am mummy.

What said that? Mummy opens her eyes and arches her back and looks all about her. She snivels and wipes the snot away from her lip. What said that? She is alone in here! Is that wretched swelling ghost come back to torment her already? This is not fair has she not suffered enough?

Not yet mummy.

WHERE ARE YOU? Mummy leaps to her feet and her thumping heart almost pulls her across the room – she really is quite beside herself now – there was barely time to let the anguish wear thin before it gave way so suddenly to utter terror.

Come on mummy where do you think I am?

I DON'T KNOW!

In Heaven of course.

WHERE IS THAT?

Work it out.

It takes surprisingly little time for mummy to work it out. Where was little baby Victor when he died? Where did he go? The Children's Hospice of course! That must be where Heaven is. That dilapidated temple of grey stone and flickering light and crushed children and dripping pipes and the constant lingering smell of rotting fish – that must be where Heaven is!

And mummy is there. Skippins (taken aback, of course) ushers her in and says I Must Say I

Wasn't Expecting To See You Again and mummy asks to see Victor and Skippins says What Do You Mean? You Know His Corpse Ain't Here and mummy says No Not His Corpse and Skippins suddenly grins a nasty grin and says Ah Ha Now You're Talking and he holds up his lantern and bounds down the corridor shouting Come With Me! No Time To Lose! And mummy trails behind him down those sorrowfully familiar corridors dodging leaks and puddles and pleading eyes behind dark doors and down and down and down past little Cindy with the bad spirit past little Alex the petrified sculpture and past little Ralph the misshapen spider-boy scuttling around in little circles and down and down to the lowest level of the dankest guts of the Children's Hospice to that terrible little door behind which little baby Victor breathed his last Earthly breath and Skippins kicks that door open with aplomb and in he goes and there is that cold slab and that bulky machine with all its wires and tubes but no baby boy to stick it to for the room is unoccupied now but the murky spotlight still shines upon the spot where Victor's brief life came to an end and beyond all that there is another little door – smaller and somehow more menacing than the first, for all its stark and featureless and – well – it's a door – what more is there to say? Mummy never noticed it last time she was here because she could never bring herself to see beyond her little baby boy (alright, she still can't). Skippins marches on and swivels on his foot to turn and face mummy and he is still grinning and he raises an index finger and beckons to mummy and asks if she is ready and mummy nods (though is uncertain) and Skippins says Good and stands to one side and shoves the little door open wide and would you ever believe what's on the other side? Flickering wild light, unending torrents of howling wind and a deafening barrage of yawning, groaning bellows rising up from a bottomless, twisted abyss of blood red and rotten, fleshy purple cascading and spiralling on through inexpressible eternity and all of this anguish and atmospheric torment howls and bolts out through the door back at mummy who clutches onto the doorframe for dear life and she can't remotely take it in – who could? It is the gateway to a world wholly unrecognisable to those who have only ever lived on ours. It is the very portrait of utter hopelessness and eternal suffering compounded and processed and spread over ungodly planes of ghastly colour and brutal, elemental onslaught and it all pours and bleeds and howls and hurricanes out through this tiny little door on the back wall of a dank box room ward in the lowest level of the darkest cellar at the end of the narrowest corridor through the most upsetting old building on planet Earth and it only appears to go on further down as far as mummy can see and as she in the torrent and tries to maintain footing she hears Skippins ask Ready To Step Inside? And without a shadow of doubt mummy nods and off she goes. Her marrow heart is crumbling between her bones but it is still just about able to nourish her courage you know.

VI

Mummy steps into the void and feels it all too suddenly as Skippins slams the door behind her. Oh he is there too of course but he is behind and mummy passes through this first ain't she brave? Into the whirlpool of horror the battering lights the vivid, visceral colour the twisting turning guts the groans the howls the thumping wind the lack of proper footing (surely health and safety never made it this far) mummy just somehow moves through it all. And down and down she goes into the very depths of this sickening realm that is all the meaner just as it is all the deeper.

Skippins the unlikely tour-guide moves along leisurely behind mummy and though he knows the way better he never feels an urge to point it out because there isn't exactly much else to explore there is only the cramped descent and that's what they are doing. All sense of space dissipates and all memory of the brickwork and the murky light and the leakages of the Children's Hospice slip to nothingness like sand through fingers and there is only this place now, whatever it is. The little door through which mummy passed is so far from view and just as relevant. Mummy descends with smiling Skippins behind her and though the omniscient groans and howls and the breath-pinching wind would seemingly have it otherwise she eventually finds the very bottom and it is like moist, uneven rock and she finds her feet there and a hungry, diseased cavern lies before her.

Get A Move On says Skippins behind mummy and mummy does just that. She can walk now and she takes one edgy footstep toward the cavern, and then a second uncertain one, then a third begrudging one, then a fourth timid one. Others are frightened, unwell, shaky, stifled and shy but they are all footsteps and they carry her into the blackness of the place she has already tonight expressed a desire to visit.

Flayed, unfed, gashed and gutted bodies cling to the walls from mucky floor to shadowy ceiling – held upright by chains and still living despite it all. Arms are stretched out at the sides and pinned to the rock walls at the wrists as flesh-clad ribcages heave and shake and twist and jaws protrude in agony and gut-wrenching screams of perpetual torture slither through the tunnels and looming shapes before these pinned up creatures clutch pikes and spikes and blades and with demonic fervour they thrust these things into the frail, sleight bodies of the screaming chained. The baying rapists forced to the walls and denied any respite shake, rattle and roll and howl as their oppressors force things into their guts which pierce and pop and offer blood and bile to the rocky ground but they do not die – they live. And the shady demons stab and thrust again and again and with clawed hands they scale the wet walls so they can offer such torment to those attached to higher levels – for there is no patch of wall left unoccupied by such men; bound, broken and unfed sinners of life all thrust to the ascension and chained there to serve as sinful nourishment to the dutiful demons who remain on hand ready to serve up an unaccountable eternity of bloody punishment. Who they were in life can not matter any more for all they know now is pain untold and unending and when pain is all there is to be known then self becomes absent – and make no mistake the pain they heaped upon the world in their former, freer lives has been repaid tenfold within the first nanoseconds of their interments to this realm, whatever it is.

Up ahead lies a festering pungent pile of matted red wet things clustered like frogspawn to the walls. Terrified eyes stare up from the severed heads – flayed and meaty at the necks – that line the corners and litter the walkways – perhaps these are the men that the demons have grown weary of torturing – they live yet of course as everyone in here must – but for now they are detached bonces simply able to stare in anguish at mummy as she passes. The walls are crudely painted with guts and gruel and phallic rocks creep up and dangle down throughout and they cut through the echoes and give chorus to the swamp of screams which never concedes in this place. Fire rises from pits all around and magma seeps from cracks in the walls and wearied, chained killers and rapists huff and puff and cry and yell but it is all in vain and mummy like the pitying charity worker passes through it all exuding sorrow and disgust but not burdened at all with the ability to act on what she sees.

Welcome To Heaven Missus.   Yeah Yeah Heaven I said I aint wrong. You wanted to see Heaven and I took you there. See Jesus ain't been home of late so Heaven's all gone a bit to pot but he's back now he's had some business to attend to and this Heaven could use some tidying up I don't wonder many might confuse it for the other place but that's really what happens when Jesus ain't been home it all goes to shit and rather quickly too.

Yeah Yeah I'm the warden like I said I'm the warden for the Hospice but that's just a front for this place where we're at now that's just a gate and this is where I really work. The hours ain't great and the pay ain't much to write home about but they look after you once you retire (us I mean, not them sorry chaps in chains). Keep on moving ignore the guts and the groans those shady things are angels like me they're just checking the sorry souls what are chained to them walls – see some of them are rapists and nonces and don't belong here so we prod 'em just to make sure. No room for them what were cunts in life here. No room at all thanks. And when we're sure they're in the wrong place we lop off their noggins and chuck 'em in a chute what does in fact lead to the other place. That's how they can't escape again see many of 'em find their way up that very chute in the first place see, demons in the other place are a dense parade of hopeless bastards if you ask me but then if working conditions down there aren't to be improved then why should the quality of work? Keep moving. I'll tell you though – you won't see a bodiless head make its way up that chute – I'd love to see one try though – scaling the chute using its tongue or its chin to hoist on up oh ha, oh ha ha ha! Deary me that's an image! Oh ha ha ha! Ooh here's another one up that chute what are they like? What's he got round his neck? Oh! You know this one – most be fresh off the belt – look at him! He was your feller weren't he? Look at his neck – must have done it himself. OI GET ON YOUR KNEES MATEY BOY I KNOW WHAT YOU ARE! HOW DARE YOU TRY AND COME HERE! BACK ON YOUR KNEES! Things must have finally gotten too much for him in that prison and he strung himself up. Well missus aren't you a pretty little bundle of convenience? No need to check this one too much because I already know what he's done. REMEMBER HER? Lord we really could do with a lock on that chute. Anyway let's take his head – DON'T MOVE – there we go. You lads can do what you want with the body and back down the chute with you my man oh the things they'll do to you down there! Have a blast matey boy!

See that was the whole family down here for a minute there. How funny! Yeah your Victor's here don't you worry he's just got home see he had some business to attend to. Your old feller's head down in that other place must be having quite a time – rape, murder and suicide! They don't even let *me* know what they do to activists of the holy three (that's what we call 'em) but I've seen some things and if *I'm* not allowed to see that then I can only imagine (but don't).

Look at this mug – him on the scaffold – want to know what he did? He's my favourite this one – Toby his name is – little baby Toby to someone once I suppose – Toby used to pick up little girls in crowded places and take them home with him very much against their wishes. What he did with 'em between then and the next bit is anyone's guess but either way he'd eventually hack their little heads off much like I just did with your old feller just there – and he'd somehow ensure they were smiling when he did it – and he'd keep 'em well looked after for a while just letting the panic and palaver build and mount and watch the televised mums and dads shake and cry and beg on the news and just when they were at the very tipping points of their own sanities he'd take the little girls' heads at night to their own front gardens and tap lightly on the windowpane and in the most convincing little girl voice you've ever heard from a burly bloke he'd say *Mummy! Daddy! Let me in please! I've come home!* And variations thereupon – and he'd poke the little smiling head up against the window so they could see their baby girl returning to them at long last and then – I suppose with skills acquired as a child from the game knock down ginger – he'd leg it into the night leaving just the head there on the lawn for the excited parents to see – held up by a thick twig planted in the earth or sometimes a big bone if he brought one with him. And he'd do that every now and then over the years always taking a little girl from a busy place, never keeping the bodies, until one dad savvy of the pattern knew exactly what to do. Frank was a scary bloke. And a tough old biscuit to boot. Once he'd accepted that his little girl wouldn't be coming home (alive at any rate) he prepared for the worst as he remembered all the previous cases. So he knew his Tiffany was gone from this world and he consoled himself to catch the killer and revenge himself. Night after night while his poor wife June was left inside alone to weep for little Tiffany Frank would sit on the opposite side of the road in a garden chair shaded by a willow. Soon as the sun went down he went there. Twenty nights went by before Frank saw the inside of his house of an evening again until he finally spied a hunched, ugly man crouched and creeping across the lawn carrying a little sack with something tiny bouncing about inside. He got up quickly as the hunched man stooped beneath his kitchen window and reached into the bag. Ideally Frank would have wanted to stop the beast before having to see what was in the bag but he wasn't quite quick enough for that. He shot up out of his chair and with a maelstrom of sense-reducing rage whirling through his blood vessels he sprinted across the road and leapt through the air at the killer (who was startled) just as he pulled little Tiffany's detached head from the sack. Frank tackled Toby to the ground and the tiny noggin was flung from his grip and careened into the window with a heavy bump and splat before dropping to the ground and rolling across the lawn – all the while still smiling. Frank – with his hands on Toby's throat – saw this and it made his grip tighten and tighten. He intended to kill Toby that day either way but the horror show that Toby accidentally played out for Frank made him do it all the quicker. Crushed his throat like a plastic carrier bag and snapped his neck like a milky bar. And then Toby found himself here. In Heaven. Hell was full at the time and we said we'd have him, said we're capable of punishing he of such fervent hobby just as well as them dickhead demons down there. Toby went to Heaven but we give him Hell here. Don't worry. Tiffany's here too of course – she never did anything wrong did she? And all them terminal kids upstairs who you met the other night, they'll be here soon too. That's what a Children's Hospice is of course – a waiting room for the afterlife. I told you that already. But Frank's going down there I imagine. Killing's a sin – whoever you kill. Them's God's rules.

Is God here? Don't ask that again. You aint snuffed it yet you're not allowed to know. You'll know when you snuff it but Lord don't ever ask me that until then! Well we're here just at the end of this cavern that shadowy place you can't make out he's in there your boy just out of sight Oi Victor! Your Mum's Here! Go on ahead you don't need me to show you any more.

And the shadow whispers *Mother?* And mummy tiptoes cautiously into it as the rotten red walls and the crooked frame of Skippins fall to darkness up ahead is the frame of a man – broad and chiselled – the finest figure of a man she ever saw and He becomes more discernable the closer mummy gets and the horrors of Heaven are no longer to be seen there is just black but He is alight and so is mummy and now it is just the two of them alight for each to behold in an eternity of darkness.

Victor looks like his daddy – but a version of daddy who never grew tired and fat and never swore allegiance to the television. His smile makes a thousand promises of loyalty and His hair is golden and falls delicately about His eyes and ears. Tears form in mummy's eyes and in disbelief (a capacity she is thankful still to possess) she gasps and covers her mouth while lovely Victor sees this and hops toward her in her aid. He takes her softly by the shoulders and He kisses her on the cheek and says Hello Mother How Have You Been?

Been better. You?

Fantastic. I've never felt so good in years.

Years? You haven't had years.

I've had many long years mother. Look how I've grown. I've lived.

Lived how? You died.

I've lived in Heaven. I'm alive in Heaven – the Heaven of invention of course. I've lived more than I ever did on your Earth. And I've been with you all the while too. They let me visit you whenever I like. That Skippins chap might not seem it but he's quite a lovely man.

He just decapitated your father.

My father had it coming.

You visit me?

All the time. Sometimes you're still awake and it seems I unsettle you a bit. Sorry about that, I don't mean to. Time in the Heaven of Invention passes differently to your time. I've lived many years in what you'd endure as just a few weeks.

I feel like I've lived a fair few years these last weeks too.

I know what you've been through and I'm sorry you have. All the comfort I can give you is that your baby boy is absolutely fine.

But this isn't real.

It's real to me.

But it's a horrible place.

It just needs a tidy up. You should see dad's house.

Fair enough. Is God here?

Don't ask that.

Is Jesus here?

He... comes and goes.

Can I stay here?

No.

Can you come back with me?

No.

Can I come back to visit you?

You will be back here one day, providing you live a good life. I lived no life, mum. I was just a toddler when death stole me. Unconscious in that horrible room upstairs. I remember every second of it, mum. They let you have your unconscious memory back when you get here. That lonely, dark room, Skippins trying to force that god-awful fish mush down my throat, you speaking to me – shouting at me!

Sorry about that.

It's okay. Dad never visited me.

I think he just tried to. But Skippins wouldn't let him.

I see.

I miss you Victor.

I love you mummy.

Mummy embraces Victor and Victor embraces mummy and she can feel his heartbeat as they hold one another and she knows then he is real and she knows he is a good man with a good heart and that he has taken the best of mummy and the best of daddy whatever that was and that he will live long and always be true and mummy knows only peace in this utterly blank realm in which she stands but soon she hears the doleful cry of Skippins behind and Victor loosens his hug and steps back and is worried it seems and mummy steps back too and is confused now and that peace didn't last all that long and Victor says Mum! Go Now! Please Go Right Now!

I don't want to!

Please go! For your sake you can't see this!

I don't want to yet! See what?

Time's Up!

And Victor clutches himself and wobbles and groans and his face begins to sag and his eyeballs sink into his skull and soon fall away and he collapses to his knees and cries and his fingers fall flaccid and he drops to the ground and writhes in agony and his skin fades to dull grey and his hair thins and falls and he wriggles and groans and mummy sees it all she probably should have gone when he said and now he is on his back his groaning jaw agape and his grey skin bubbles and seeps and begins to run and falls loose and peels away from his bones which shrink and shrink as the skin comes away and fades into the dark – no blood or guts lie beneath them – just the contracting skeleton that is all there is now – just a tiny little pile of baby bones on the ground at mummy's feet – and here is Skippins again and he sees the bones too and he nods solemnly and says Yeah That Does Happen. And mummy is crying again and Skippins pats her on the back with commiseration. I'll Show You Out Missus.

And she is out. There is no trek through the snarling caves of Heaven, no ramble up the dark and staring corridors of the Children's Hospice and certainly no soggy jog through the forests that surround the place. Lance is left to his fish without interruption. Mummy is at home again – standing in the front room with the dusty Christmas tree the quiet piano and the little piano stool which has little baby Victor inside. She stares a long while at that little stool which looks more and more – the longer she beholds it – like a stout little four-legged monster which has eaten up her baby and is now snarling threateningly at her. What a thing! Mummy hates it now! Her poor little baby boy – he's not a thriving, beautiful man living a fruitful life – he's a rotting little corpse encased in a rabid hound of leather and wood. What a day! He's right there – right inside there right now – not blinking or breathing or growing or smiling – he's in there right now turning shrivelled and grey and getting smelly inside that stool and as this reality continues to torment her the doorbell rings and mummy ignores it so it rings again and mummy answers it.

There is nobody there. Yes there is. Mummy looks down and there is the one she forgot all about and who she might have seen at little baby Victor's funeral the adorable the fluffy the wagging the loyal the warm the Christmas puppy yay!

So mummy bends down to greet this little hairball of consolation she tickles his ear and strokes his fur and says Little Puppy I've Missed You Who's A Good Boy Then Yes You Are The Best Boy Yes You Are.

Now, Now, says the Christmas puppy in headmasterly tones. I haven't time for this my dear I must come in. Would you kindly prepare me a bowl of tap water? For I've been wandering these streets for weeks and I am ever so tired and thirsty. And I have not tasted meat nor have I bitten or barked – thank you. Also I must apologise for this but you never bothered to try and house train me so I shall leave this here and you can clean it up later if you wish.

I couldn't return to this place sooner than tonight. I have spectacular information for you and only now are you ready to know it. As you may have guessed already I never really abandoned you and Victor. I wanted no part in a household run by a violent abuser of women so I fled on that night as any decent dog would have done. But I kept a concerned eye on the two of you since then. I ventured up to the Children's Hospice from time to time – ah, thank you for the water – to see poor Victor before his passing. That man Skippins was strange but very kind. I sat by Victor's side nightly and he spoke to me. Please don't be surprised, we understood one another very well. He told me he knew that he wasn't long for this world and I told him to be at peace. I told him he was going to see the Gods and he expressed concern that they might not like him. I assured him that they will. He was a good little boy and no God could ever turn him away. I attended his lonely funeral but I remained at the gate so you wouldn't see me (the time wasn't right) but I believe you saw me though I was largely unconcerned as my presence didn't seem to be of much interest to you.

Now my wanderings have come to their end. I have returned to you because you called me loyal before and loyal I am. Though I wish you would stop calling me puppy for I am two years old now and I have gained a wealth of knowledge and experience in that time. Like you, I am a genius. Unlike you, I shall never be able to prove it so. But my life is unimportant and I don't mope about it. I am here to reiterate: You are a genius. And you can still prove it. You went to Heaven this evening yes? You saw Victor as a man yes? He told you he is alive yes? Well he isn't. Not yet. You are a genius – you bore the Second Coming. Clever. Victor is our Lord and Saviour returned to us. But what a world this is! You aborted the Second Coming before he could teach us things and you looked your abortion in the eye as you did so. Few are allowed that privilege. The Saviour of Man must now be saved by a woman. And only you have the power to do this. The Victor you met tonight is the Victor that will be born again if you take hold of your courage and strength and allow this to happen. The Heaven you saw dressed as Hell is the realm He must revive but only when He has revived the Earth can He do that. You must give Him life. Man is the Creator but also the destroyer. Man destroyed himself. Woman is the giver of life and seldom the brute force and here she is alive and well! Release this power and give the world what it so desperately needs in this age. Keep Christmas in your heart the way you have kept it in your living room (but be sure to keep dusting) and return its most blessed light to life now. Time is of the essence! The longer you wait the less likely it is that our Lord and Salvation will emerge the Victor. Since that dreaded night you have been led around by men and men have not let you speak so now roar!

And upon his final word the Christmas puppy crouches to the ground before the water bowl and laps it dry and wags his tail and then patters over to the settee and leaps onto it to take a well-earned nap and what is mummy to do now? She is free now. The overbearing men can command her no more. She is the king of her destiny now – Christmas puppy is right. Oh wise little doggy! Such a clever little boy! You'll be getting the very best doggy treats from now on!

And *Jesus.*

Maybe my marrow heart will get the better of me! Maybe the muscle – the vessel – the withered pulsing hunk of meat – will finally let me sleep! That piano stool is no longer a threatening beast, it is a treasure chest of hope itching to be opened. And mummy makes for it with the urgency that Christmas puppy has given to her. It is still Christmas in this house and here is mummy finally opening her Christmas present. The lovely tree stands watch the shiny tinsel the greeting cards the bells the twinkling lights the smiling Santas the pink Elephant (what *was* nan thinking?) the baubles red gold and silver the Christmas star the dangling chocolate snowmen the wrapping paper the Christmas puppy snoozing on the settee tinsel fire cake pretty bow God Bless Us Dickens Grinch Carols and Christmas Cheer and Goodwill To All Men and To Man's Best Friend warm warm merry merry Christmas puppy yay! And mummy's present is opened the seat of the stool lies on the carpet with all the wrapping paper and there is her treasure her boy her joy a greater melody than ever she created on that piano. He looks different now – he is grey-green and wrinkled and there's a bit of a rancid smell which greets mummy as little baby Victor is revealed but it's not too much and mummy knows that for little baby Victor to be born again then he must be back inside her so she swiftly turns over various means of going about this and comes to the most sensible before long. This should work, she has been so occupied recently and it only occurs to her now just how ravenous mummy is so she takes hold of her baby and attempts to remove him from his box but the flesh is soft and weak and it comes away from his body with surprising ease and mummy holds the shred of skin up in front of her eyes pondering it for a moment and then without further ado she places it on her tongue and chomps it down and it tastes foul and it makes her gag but she has a job to do and once it is down inside her she hoists the baby boy out of his box and on her knees she puts him on the floor and she takes more loose flesh and down it goes and she does so again and gags and sometimes heaves but she carries on taking bigger servings with each turn and eventually ceasing to discriminate against bone too so she crunches bits of that down to bulk out the meal. Ravenous, hopeful mummy pulls at little baby Victor – whole limbs at a time now – and what is left of him before her now is scarcely recognisable and the rotten meat hurts her guts and the bone cuts at her throat and she feels a rising sickness but does not give up. She expresses love and promise at the incomplete, misshapen Victor between mouthfuls and the sickness rises and rises and the mouthfuls clog her throat and the heaviness sets in her head as it has done in her tummy and it is blinding and fatiguing and she fails to remain upright but it's okay because little baby Victor is all gone now all inside mummy ready to be born anew oh what joy is approaching! Little baby Christmas Rudolph picture postcard tinsel snow and cakes dusty dusty cakes warm fire pretty bow and tinsel tinsel tinsel fire cake and fucking wine elves Santa cheerful little Christmas baby smiles and songs and here he comes little baby Victor all grown up coming home in the cold here he comes he's at the door oh my he's so close a big strong man at the door now the light leaves mummy's eyes but Christmas puppy awakens suddenly and barks at the doorbell and wags and leaps from the settee sweet dreams mummy here he comes little baby Christmas born again come to save us all and isn't about bloody time?

Printed in Great Britain
by Amazon.co.uk, Ltd.,
Marston Gate.